Bartholomew the Champion

Bartholomew the Champion

Steve Attridge

Collins
An imprint of HarperCollins*Publishers*

by Steve Attridge

Bartholomew the Champion
Trash Cat's Secret

And coming soon

Toffee's Big Problem
Thumper the Brave

For my son, Jacob. Also, thanks to staff at the Avonvale Veterinary Group, Warwick, for their help. Any factual errors remain mine alone.

First published in Great Britain 1996
by Collins

3 5 7 9 8 6 4

Collins is a division of
HarperCollins*Publishers* Ltd
77-85 Fulham Palace Road, London W6 8JB

ISBN 000-675242-X

Printed and bound in Great Britain by
Caledonian International Book Manufacturing Ltd, Glasgow, G 64

Chapter One

EMERGENCY

Eddie wiped Hannibal's wet slobber from his face and laughed. He would much rather be kissed by Hannibal the bulldog than by any of his aunts and uncles, but there was work to be done.

"Come on, boy," he said, patting the old dog's head. Hannibal, whose back legs had been crushed in an awful road accident, now had a very splendid chariot attached to him and he propelled himself along using his powerful front legs. The wheels squeaked, so you always knew when he was coming. Everyone at the Rainbow Animal Hospital had grown to love old Hannibal. For some reason Eddie couldn't fathom, his owner didn't want him back, so the dog would probably be a long-stay patient. He was Eddie's special mate, and always accompanied him on his rounds of the hospital. They weren't official rounds, given that Eddie was eleven years old and it would be some years before he became a proper vet, but there wasn't an inch of the hospital he didn't know, especially since his sister, Chelsea, had got the job of receptionist.

Every afternoon after school Eddie

was there, much to the annoyance of one of the vets, Mr Wensleydale, or *Old Cheesy* as Eddie called him. Old Cheesy told Eddie he was like a flea – always there and never wanted. Eddie considered there were worse things than being a flea – like being a grumpy old bloke called Wensleydale, but he didn't say that. He just tried to keep out of Old Cheesy's way as much as possible.

Eddie continued his rounds through one of the wards. Cats in cages. Dogs in cages. Spock the bad-tempered seagull stomping up and down the cage on his splinted leg like Long John Silver, spitting and cursing his bad luck, thought Eddie. A cat with its ear bandaged after a fight, probably now day-dreaming about cream and revenge. The wonderful smell of fur and hay in the room. Eddie stopped and helped Greg clean out one of the cages. Greg was one of the nursing assistants.

"Anything new?" Eddie asked. Greg smiled. Greg was all right. Even if he did have a dopey pony-tail. If he passed his exams in the summer he would become a fully qualified veterinary nurse, so Eddie knew he had to be pretty intelligent.

"Not yet, but you never know," Greg said, as Eddie, followed by Hannibal, disappeared into the storeroom to check supplies and to breathe in the smell of animal feed and disinfectant. As long as there was plenty of food and bedding Eddie felt everything was under control. There was nothing that couldn't be coped with at the hospital. His hospital. Well, in a way it was his. After all, he knew as much about what went on there as anyone else. He even found Hannibal's slobbery wheezing interesting. It sounded like seagulls with sore throats singing to an old pair of squeaking bagpipes. Real music. And the short-bristled coat that always went back to its perfect black and white patch formation, no matter how much you stroked it the other way. Eddie gave Hannibal a hug goodbye outside the storeroom and walked along the corridor to the consulting rooms.

One of the doors was open and there was Hilary David, the other hospital vet, bending over a tortoise, bathing its eyes with a piece of cotton wool soaked in warm water. Eddie peered in and had a good idea that the tortoise was having trouble waking up after hibernation and its eyes were sticky. He'd read about it somewhere – one of the millions of bits of information he stored away like a squirrel stored its winter nuts.

Reception was its usual bustle of ringing telephones, nurses coming and going with animals, people with their pets waiting to see a vet, and always the possibility of the unexpected. Posters adorned the walls:

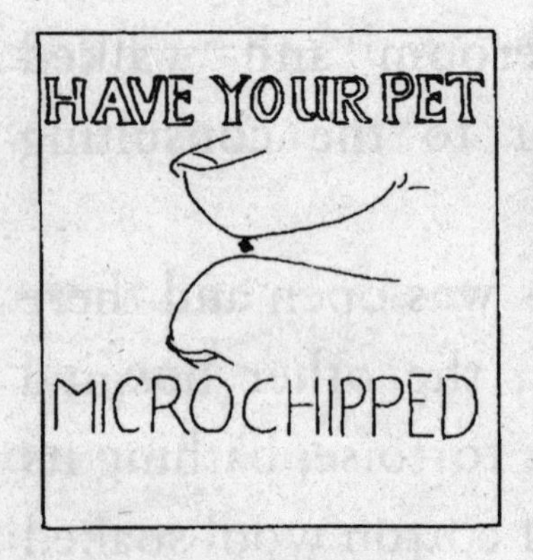

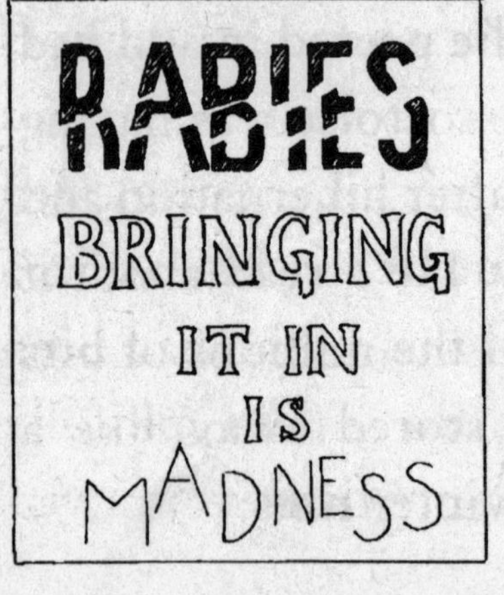

This last poster had horrendous enlarged pictures of disgusting things, including tapeworms with triffid-like heads that can live inside some animals. Eddie always made himself look at it so that when he became a vet, nothing would disgust him when he had to treat animals.

There was one wall that Eddie particularly liked. It was a gallery of photographs taken by grateful people whose pets had been helped at the hospital: Gordon the gerbil who had successfully recovered from a stomach operation and now peered curiously at the camera, wondering what all the fuss was about; Jasper the rabbit who got his head stuck in a flower pot in the garden but now sat contentedly in his owner's lap; Jenny the greyhound who had been savaged by another dog and was pitifully showing the scar on her flank as if it was

a war wound, which it was in a way.

Eddie thought none of those people knew how lucky they were to have pets. If only he . . . but it wasn't worth going through all that again. Pigs would fly before his mum and dad lifted their NO PETS ban.

Eddie was just about to snoop along the line of new patients to see what they were when Chelsea beckoned him over to the Reception desk.

"What is it?" Eddie asked.

"In the private waiting room. In the aquarium. We think it's male. Be careful," Chelsea warned him.

Eddie went behind her desk and through into the small private waiting room. It was usually reserved for "difficult patients" such as dogs who were so fed up with the world and themselves that they were either terrified or aggressive, sometimes both, and had to be kept on their own until a vet was free to attend to them. On a shelf at the back of the room was an aquarium with plants in it and a little light inside. On the front a label read: *Mexican red-kneed tarantula*. A tarantula! Eddie peered closely. Gravel, moss, bits of wood, and there in the shadows, watching, was the spider, faint red blushes on his legs, as if he had fallen and hurt all his knees at once. It was tempting to tap the glass and see what the spider would do, but Eddie liked to think that creatures had their own thoughts and wishes, and if they wanted to be left to themselves in the shadows, then that was their business. Anyway, for the spider to be here, there had to be something wrong with it.

"I'll call you . . . Miguel," whispered Eddie, his breath frosting the glass.

"Si, si, Señor Eddie, you are one good hombre," Eddie replied to himself in what he imagined was a pretty good Mexican accent.

Then, from Reception he heard urgency in Chelsea's voice as she spoke to the ambulance driver on his mobile phone.

"OK, Ron. We'll be ready. Two minutes," said Chelsea.

An emergency! Eddie both hated and was excited by emergencies. He didn't yet know – for how could he? – that this particular emergency was going to make his own life a great deal more complicated.

Chapter Two
The New Arrival

"What is it? What have you got? What's wrong?" Eddie called as he ran towards the front entrance.

Kalim, a veterinary nurse, was already at the big glass-fronted double doors, securing them open. Chelsea was helping her. People sitting with their pets in

Reception watched in anticipation.

Eddie ran outside to be the first to greet the ambulance. And here it was with Ron at the wheel, his ferrety face fixed in concentration as he pulled up and got out. Eddie was already opening the rear doors. Inside it was much like an ambulance for humans, except that the seat parts were lower and there were cages and animal carriers.

"Careful, lad, he's a big'un," warned Ron.

"What's wrong with him?" asked Eddie.

The doors were fully open and there, on a stretcher, was one of the biggest dogs Eddie had ever seen. A Bernese Mountain Dog with a head the size of a lion's and a thick black, brown and white coat. A dog that could probably eat a hundred hamburgers between meals. It was a dog Eddie recognised. He stepped aside as Kalim wheeled the trolley up to the back of the ambulance so that the stretcher could be slid onto it. He was about to jump into the ambulance to help Ron when a large hand with a little forest of hairs on the back and wearing a gold ring, gripped his shoulder.

"Oh no you don't!" said Mr Wensleydale, scowling at Eddie. "I've told you before – no getting in the way." Then the vet turned to Ron to ask him what was wrong.

"Broken leg, Mr Wensleydale. And he seems to have gone into shock."

By now, the dog was on the trolley and being wheeled into the hospital at great speed. Eddie followed behind, listening.

"Operating room," directed Mr Wensleydale. "I don't like the look of him."

"Hilary has a cat in the operating room," said Kalim.

"Emergency room, then," snapped Mr Wensleydale.

Eddie decided that if ever he became rich he would use his money to build a second operating theatre for the Animal Hospital.

Doors were flung wide open and the trolley pushed quickly into the emergency room. Mr Wensleydale decided to leave the huge dog on the trolley. The dog's eyes flickered and rolled, then closed again. Mr Wensleydale listened to the heart beat and Eddie repeated to himself over and over again, "Keep going, keep going, keep going." The vet then opened the dog's mouth. The tongue, as big as a size seven shoe, was a nasty bluish colour and very dry.

"Do you want to set the leg?" Kalim asked.

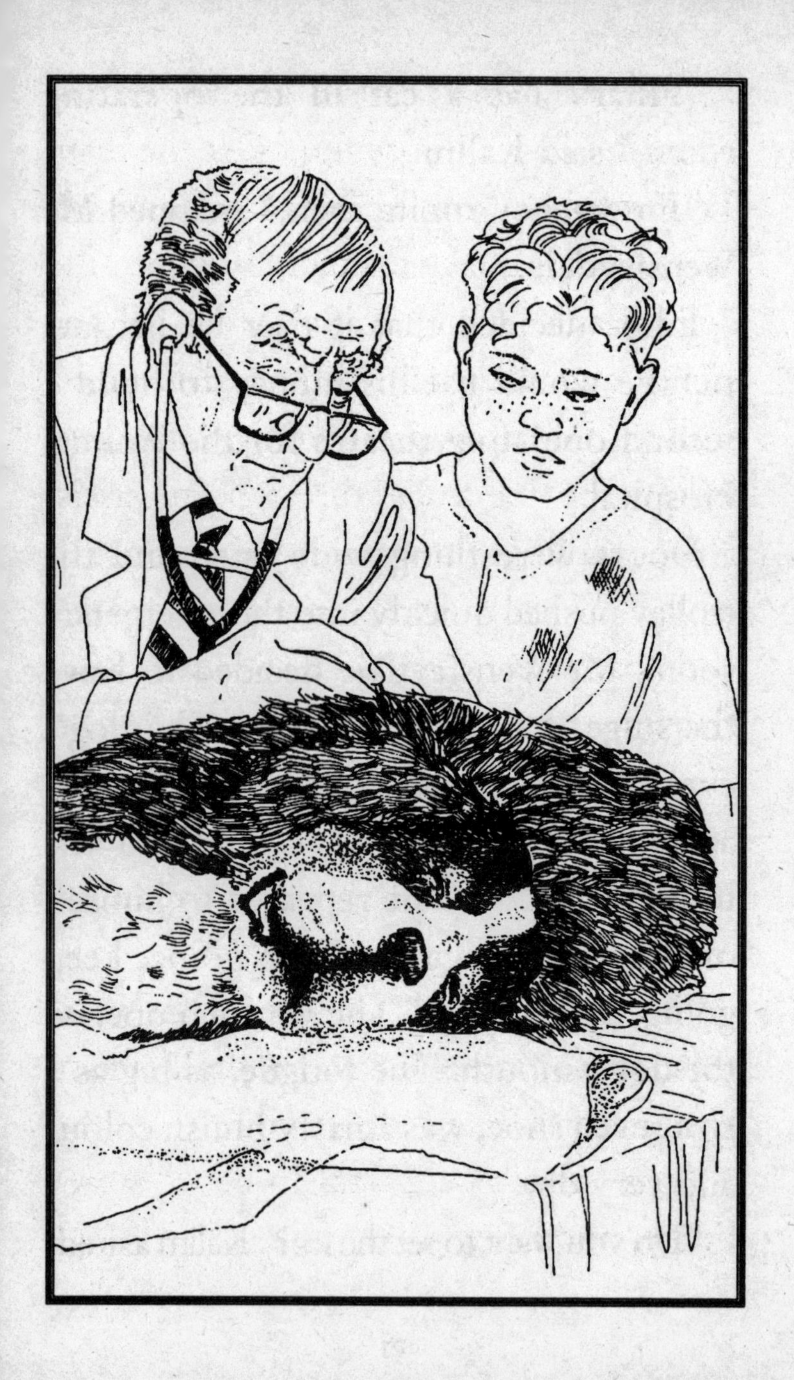

"Not yet. We've got to get some fluid into him, or we'll lose him. Get the drip. This will help the leg for now," and Mr Wensleydale injected a painkiller into the dog's flank, while Kalim went to the stores and returned with a drip on a trolley. Eddie was frowning hard and willing the dog to get through this crisis. His breathing was raspy and painful to hear.

"What happened?" Eddie asked Ron, knowing he should keep quiet while Old Cheesy was around but unable to contain his curiosity. Mr Wensleydale shot him a "Shut up!" glare and attended to the drip.

"Bit daft, really. You know he's the mascot for the local football team, Lymington United, don't you?"

"His name's Bartholomew," said Eddie, nodding.

Ron continued. "Well, they were out training and some big presentation lunch was waiting for them when they finished. Only they never got it because this big fella got up on the table and snaffled half of it. Then the table broke. He landed awkwardly and broke his leg. Nasty one. By the time I got there he'd passed out."

"I've seen him at home matches," said Eddie. "They call him Big Belly Bart because he's got this mega appetite. And he's . . . "

"All right, all right! I don't need a whole life history. And in any case, what on earth do you think you're doing in here?" hissed Mr Wensleydale.

"Just . . . trying to help," said Eddie.

"I'll tell you exactly how you can help once I've finished this," said the vet as he examined the dog again and adjusted the drip. "OK, Kalim. Now the leg."

Eddie watched, fascinated, as the dog's big front leg was lifted and examined, the break found, set and held, then splinted while Kalim was sent to get plaster bandages for the cast. Because Bartholomew was such a large dog, Mr Wensleydale was worried that the leg might give way when he put his weight on it. The cast was to give extra support. At last it was finished and, wiping a few drops of sweat from his forehead, Mr Wensleydale turned to Eddie.

"I'm afraid this is it for you, young man," he said. "You have no right to be in this hospital, getting under people's feet, bothering owners when their pets are sick. If anything were to happen to you or to one of the animals because of you, I'd be the one held responsible."

"I'll keep quiet in future," Eddie promised. "Quiet as a mouse, careful as a cat, helpful as a sheepdog. You won't even know I'm here."

"Exactly. Because as from today – I am banning you from this hospital!" said Mr Wensleydale.

Chapter Three
Goodbye for Now

Eddie's eyes filled with tears, but he wasn't going to let Mr Wensleydale see that. Not in a million years. Eddie rushed from the emergency room and down the corridor into the main ward. He went straight to Hannibal, who was having a good doze, dreaming for all we know of winning a chariot race in the film of *Ben Hur*. Eddie fell onto him, clasping him around the neck.

"Old Cheesy says I can't come here any more."

Hannibal opened one eye and gave Eddie a very large slurping lick, starting at his chin and ending up on the top of his head. It instantly made Eddie feel better. It was true that Eddie had no right to be at the hospital, at least no right that Old Cheesy would understand. At first he had come with friends who had pets, then he'd stop by to walk home with Chelsea, and before long, without anyone properly knowing how or when it had happened, Eddie was a fixture. He belonged there. He knew that. Unfortunately, Old Cheesy-breath didn't quite see it the same way, and it was his opinion that counted.

Eddie turned his mind to the more immediate problem of Bartholomew.

"Listen, there's a new dog. Bartholomew. Broken leg and in shock. Be dead nice to him, won't you, Han?"

Hannibal listened intently and grunted.

"Yes. I'll try to come back. Somehow," Eddie murmured.

Hannibal gave another grunt.

"Yes, I know it's unfair, but what can I do? He works here. And he's an adult."

Eddie gave Hannibal a last hug and went round saying goodbye, at least for now, to the animals. Even Spock the bad-tempered seagull stopped shrieking and spitting his contempt at the world for a moment to focus his beady eyes on Eddie as he stopped at the cage and said, "See you, grotbags."

Eddie stood in the middle of the ward.

"Listen, everyone. I'm off for a bit, and while I'm away, no major fighting, no sulking, and no pinching each other's food." This last remark was for Hannibal.

Greg hurried in to prepare one of the cages for Bartholomew and Eddie automatically started to help him.

"Bad news?" asked Greg.

"Could say that," said Eddie and, without looking at him in case the tears returned, he told him that Old Cheesy had banned him.

Eddie quite liked Greg, except for his pony-tail and the fact that he played heavy metal tapes on his Walkman. While Eddie was still delaying the moment of leaving, Greg looked thoughtful and went downstairs to have a word with Hilary David, the other veterinary surgeon at the hospital.

* * *

Eddie walked home with Chelsea. His feet dragged and he looked back at the hospital, the entrance lights coming on as evening darkened the roads. It never closes, he thought. It never knows what will happen. No one does. Not even Mr Wensleydale, whatever he might think.

"Penny for your thoughts," said Chelsea.

"Cost you more than that. Two quid at least," replied Eddie with a bit of his usual sparkle returning.

"I can guess. Mr Wensleydale. You being barred from the hospital. Don't worry, Ed."

Eddie scowled. Why did adults say things like that? The rottenest, worst, most indescribably bad thing happens and they say, "Don't worry". But they were always worrying, mostly about dumb things, like meals and shopping, what the Government is doing, the price of petrol, and what Chelsea called *relationships.* At least Kate, his little sister, wouldn't say anything as naff as, "Don't worry".

Eddie could tell that Chelsea was about to say something else, so he asked what it was. She tapped the side of her nose confidentially. Eddie wasn't in the mood to play games, so he stuck his hands in his pockets and walked on in silence.

Kate was in her room, because she'd been grounded by their mum and dad for fighting in school again. Kate was only seven, but already she'd made her mark in the playground as someone you didn't take lightly. Because she was so small and had freckles and curly hair that looked like an exploded brillo pad, adults thought she was sweet and other children thought she was a pushover. Both were wrong. She was as tough as a tiger tooth and wasn't scared of anyone. That day she'd pulverised a nine-year-old boy who had stolen her chocolate bar. Because their mum and dad still wouldn't allow Eddie to have a pet – too expensive, too much trouble, the problem of going away – Eddie considered that having an extremely intelligent little sister was the next best thing.

She sat on her bed and considered the problem of Wensleydale.

"Sounds like you two have a difficult professional relationship," she said.

"Too right. He hates me," said Eddie. "What do you think I should do?"

Kate had a way of sometimes knowing

exactly what to do. Often, she even seemed to know what was going to happen. She did get things badly wrong, too – like when she told their mum and dad what National Lottery numbers to choose and she didn't get one right. But Eddie still had faith in her.

"I don't think you'll have to do anything. Someone else will. And I reckon you'll find a new friend who's a good listener."

Eddie didn't know whether Kate got her information by some sort of magic, from aliens, or she just knew things, but he did know that she was always worth listening to. Eddie went to bed much happier, and had one of his best dreams ever. He was a dog who could turn into a sort of superdog called Mightymutt who flew around the world saving animals from disasters and biting the trouser bottoms of villains, all of whom seemed to resemble Mr Wensleydale.

Chapter Four

EDDIE'S RETURN

The next day at about 4.30 p.m. Chelsea looked up from her desk and through the window. She smiled and picked up the internal telephone.

"Hilary? Chelsea in Reception. He's here. Right. I'll tell him. And thanks a lot."

Outside the hospital, on the other side of the road, standing under a lamppost in the rain, getting soaked, was Eddie. He was trying to look as if he just happened to be there, doing nothing in particular.

Chelsea opened the window and yelled out his name. He turned and she beckoned him over. He looked around, then made a "Who? Me?" gesture and she nodded.

Seconds later Eddie was there, dripping in Reception.

"What is it?" he asked, looking around furtively in case Mr Wensleydale was about.

"I thought you might be hanging around after school," said Chelsea.

"Just happened to be passing," said Eddie nonchalantly.

"Sure you were," said Chelsea, "but anyway, Hilary David wants to see you."

Eddie looked at his sister, but she obviously wasn't going to tell him what all this was about.

"What about Old Cheesy?" asked Eddie.

"Mr Wensleydale isn't in this afternoon. Go on. Hilary's waiting."

"Right. But first things first. How's Miguel?"

"Who?"

"The red-kneed tarantula."

"The same. Not moving. He's upstairs. In the side room," said Chelsea.

"And Bartholomew?"

"Very sorry for himself."

"Won't be long," said Eddie, darting away and through the door.

"Eddie! The vet's waiting for you."

But Fast Eddie was gone.

Because the side room had no windows,

the light was always on and the room had a musty, unreal feel to it. Eddie made straight for the aquarium that housed Miguel. He looked deep inside, searching for the spider. At last, he saw it, crouched absolutely still under one of the plants. Eddie knew Miguel was looking at him. What was wrong with him? What had happened? How did you make spiders well again?

"Hello, Miguel. I'm Eddie."

"Si. Hello amigo," he answered himself.

For a moment, it seemed to Eddie as if the glass was dissolving and he was being drawn into the aquarium. It was as if it were the whole world. He was in there, stalking through the dark shadows of the undergrowth, breathing in the weedy warmth that smelt like the inside of a steamy greenhouse on a hot day. He

could hear the rasp-rasp of Miguel's breathing . . .

Something tugged at Eddie's leg. He turned, and as he did so the world slipped back into place and there was Hannibal, his great jaws clamped on Eddie's jeans to claim his friend's attention. Much slobbering and stroking and giggling later, Hannibal led Eddie into the ward and up to the biggest cage. Bartholomew lay listlessly on the white regulation hospital mat, his plastered leg jutting out like some peculiar sword. His eyes were closed but Eddie suspected he wasn't asleep. Hannibal licked one of Bartholomew's large floppy ears. The big dog opened one eye, seemed to see nothing, and closed it again.

"I see the problem, Han," said Eddie. "Still, it's early days. Give him time."

There was a bowl of biscuits,

untouched, beside Bartholomew. Hannibal munched a few – just to encourage the other dog, of course.

In her office, Hilary David was still waiting. She rang through to Reception.

"Where is he?" she was about to ask Chelsea, but put down the telephone as the door opened and Eddie's grinning face appeared. He had been distracted outside in the corridor by Kalim carrying a kitten that had both its ears bandaged. Kalim was taking it to be weighed. Eddie thought the kitten looked female, and he knew she needed to be weighed so that Kalim could gauge the right amount of drugs to give her. Probably antibiotics to stave off infection. He wanted go with them to find out what had happened to the kitten, but now he was here, he'd better see what Hilary wanted first.

She shook her head as he came in.

"Eddie. Fifteen minutes is a long time for a boy with your energy to walk ten metres from Reception to my office."

"Friends to see," said Eddie, looking around the room. He liked Hilary David. Her room was interesting too. There was a poster of a dog's skeleton, the long spinal column tapering down into the tail; Jones' Medical Dictionary; training videos; books on vertebrates, on insects, on mammals, books with titles he didn't understand . . . not yet anyway. And on her desk, she had a collection of miniature porcelain animals and birds: an elk, a bear, a fox, a swan, a duck. It was a room that belonged to someone. Whereas, Mr Wensleydale's Spartan room with its smooth white walls and uncluttered surfaces was bare and clinical – it told you nothing about the person who used it.

"You're probably wondering why I called you in," said the vet.

"Because of my brilliant personality and handsome face?" asked Eddie, grinning widely. No point in being modest. Especially when you've been barred from a place and you've got nothing to lose.

"There is that, of course. But I was also wondering if you would do me a big favour."

Eddie paid attention. This was starting to sound interesting.

"Do you like rabbits?"

"Do I like rabbits?!" Eddie repeated incredulously. What a dopey question, he thought. Of course I do. I love rabbits. I love them almost as much as I love dogs. I think rabbits are wonderful. Rabbits, like a lot of animals, are my favourite kind of people. But all he said was, "Yes".

Hilary reached under her desk and brought out a box. Inside was a beautiful baby black and white Dutch rabbit. His large, round, aquamarine eyes peered up cautiously at Eddie, whose heart instantly melted. He put out his hand very carefully and the rabbit licked his fingers.

"Do you like him?" Hilary asked.

"He's the most beautiful rabbit I've ever seen. Baby Dutch. About four weeks old, if that," said Eddie. "Why is he here? What's wrong with him?"

"He was left this morning on the hospital steps in a cardboard box. He's weak. I've given him some antibiotics because I think he has a chest infection. But with regular feeds, at least four times a day, and a great deal of affection, I think he might pull round. Which is where you come in."

Eddie looked up at her. What was she getting at?

Chapter Five

The New Friend

"What do you mean?" asked Eddie.

"You know what it's like here, Eddie. We're understaffed, there are more cases than we can deal with. Every contribution counts. It would be a great help to me, to the hospital, if you would take responsibility for the rabbit. If you did, I'd consider you to be his official foster parent. For as long as he's here."

Eddie's eyes widened. Mr Wensleydale had barred him from the hospital. He knew that. Hilary knew that. But here she was saying that he could come in four times a day to look after the rabbit. No point in looking a gift rabbit in the mouth.

"You bet!" Eddie said. "But . . . will there be any trouble? You know, me being here?"

"Trouble!" Hilary repeated, knowing perfectly well what he meant. "I certainly hope not, Eddie."

Eddie beamed. One in the eye for Old Cheesy.

"When shall I start?"

"How about right now?" said Hilary. "You can go and sort out some bedding and a place in the ward. Get to know him. What will you call him?"

Eddie looked at the baby rabbit.

"Thumper," he said.

Greg helped Eddie to prepare a small rabbit hutch. Eddie drew up a list of food for Thumper. Dry food from the stores, then every day he'd bring in something special: carrots, lettuce, greens, cabbage, parsley, dandelion leaves. He'd come in before school, at lunchtime, then for a long stay after school with two feeds. It meant he'd miss playground football at lunchtime, but his mates would understand, and anyway, it wasn't a difficult decision to make. He could still make training one day a week, which meant he would probably keep his place in the football team.

Eddie cuddled the little rabbit against his chest and whispered, "Your name's

Thumper. You're here. With me. You're going to be all right now. You're really going to be all right." He put his face close to the rabbit and got a lick from the tiny tongue. It felt slightly dry, like being tickled with a wiry feather. Thumper's ears felt like silk – soft, creamy. Eddie planted a small kiss on Thumper's nose and the rabbit twitched his whiskers, as if he was about to sneeze.

Snuffling and grunting from behind reminded Eddie that he had other responsibilities. Hannibal, whose pungent breath and fearsome features suggested, to some people, a dangerous and repellent character, in fact never had a bad thought in him. He immediately accepted Thumper with only the merest twinge of jealousy that dissolved as Eddie hugged him, and gave him one of the emergency biscuits he often carried with him. Everything was back to normal when Eddie put Thumper in his cage and joined Hannibal to do their rounds.

The bad news was that Bartholomew hadn't eaten a thing and had only taken a few sips of water since being admitted. Greg and Eddie knelt down beside him and Eddie stroked the huge dog's head. As before, Bartholomew lazily opened one eye, then closed it again. He just didn't seem interested in the world.

"Why is he still like this?" asked Eddie.

Greg sighed.

"Could be he's in delayed shock. Perhaps the leg is causing a lot of pain. Usually, we'd expect to see some improvement by now. The problem is, if he doesn't start eating he's going to get weaker. He's got a big body to maintain."

Greg hurried off to attend to Spock, who was shrieking madly, perhaps because he was hungry or thirsty, or just plain mad at everyone and everything.

"Good boy," said Eddie, as he stroked Bartholomew's giant head. It smelt almost like a puppy's, warm and sweet, like fresh baked bread. Hannibal, whose head even Eddie would have to admit smelt more like socks before washing day, licked the dog's ear and tried to encourage him to eat by taking a few more of his biscuits. It was a generous thing to do. In fact, Hannibal had been so generous that all of Bartholomew's biscuits had now gone.

"What's up, Bartholomew?" Eddie asked, but the sick dog didn't seem to hear. Eddie would have to give this problem some serious thought. But first, he just had to go and see Thumper again. He took the little rabbit out and felt his heart beating against his hand and the whiskers twitching. Thumper licked Eddie's hand.

"You see, Bartholomew isn't eating. It's almost as if he's given up or something. But why should he? He's a brilliant big dog who's a star at the local football club. I've seen him prancing about like he's Michael Jackson." Eddie stopped. Thumper was sitting on his hand looking up intently at him, his ears sharply pointed, as if he was hanging on every word Eddie was saying. What was it Kate had said? "I reckon you'll find a new friend who's a good listener." That was it. Eddie had found the new friend all right. And Thumper's ears were made for a lot of listening. Clever old Kate. He might even tell her, although she'd probably get a swollen head over it. Nothing wrong with that if you were right, Eddie thought. He knew a lot of people with big heads and they were as thick as a kilo of turnips.

Chapter Six

The Great Argument

At night the pace of the hospital slowed down a little, though there were still animals needing round the clock attention, and emergencies didn't stop just because the working day was meant to be over. It was 8.00 p.m. and Hilary David would be on duty for another four hours. She was in the side room and had Miguel's aquarium on the table. She put on some protective gloves and lifted off the lid. There was no movement inside. There hadn't been since Miguel arrived. It was very worrying. There was a quick knock on the door and Eddie burst in.

"Eddie! I thought you went home hours ago."

"Just came in to see Miguel before I go. Thumper's the most excellent rabbit in existence. What are you doing?"

"Going to try to get some nutrition into him . . . Miguel – yes, that's a good name."

"Won't he try to bite or anything?" asked Eddie.

"The gloves will protect me. Someone from a zoo is coming to collect him in a few days, but we have to do something before then."

Hilary reached in and, very gently, lifted the spider out of the aquarium. Eddie noticed that she lifted Miguel from underneath, taking his body weight in her hand very slowly. He squatted in her hand, tensing slightly. Then she put him on the table. Eddie was fascinated. He'd never been this close to a tarantula without there being a pane of glass between him and it. Eddie moved to get a closer look and Miguel tensed, almost like a fist clenching.

"No sudden movements, Eddie," said Hilary.

"I can see his jaws," said Eddie.

"They're very powerful. You'd know it if he bit you."

"Would it kill me?"

"No, but it would be very unpleasant. He doesn't look as if he's in much of a mood for biting though."

"What do you think is wrong with him?" Eddie wanted to know.

"His body is far too light. My guess is that somebody bought him as an exotic pet without bothering to find out how to care for him properly – diet, temperature, and so on. Then they just dumped him here when he stopped moving and therefore stopped being interesting. I think he's so run down that his system won't take food in the normal way. I'm going to try to stimulate movement, then interest in food. Look."

On the table were a few dead grasshoppers and a jar of honey. Hilary took a spoonful of honey and put a little on the insects.

"Why are you doing that?" Eddie asked.

"Just experimenting," said the vet. "I'm not an expert on arachnids, but anything is worth a try."

She held one of the grasshoppers close to Miguel. Eddie leaned forward. He felt sure the spider was interested, but he didn't take the bait.

"He probably won't feed while I'm holding him, but I have to try to get him interested. I've no idea if it will work. How's Bartholomew?"

"Not good," said Eddie. "Let's hope he improves tomorrow."

"But *you* won't be here to see it if he does," said a voice behind Eddie.

Hilary and Eddie turned to see Mr Wensleydale in the doorway. Eddie could tell by the little pinkish spots under his eyes that he was angry – very angry.

"What exactly are you doing here? Are you deaf? Didn't I say that you were not to come to my hospital any more? Do you always do the exact opposite of what people tell you?"

"Er, which question shall I answer first?" asked Eddie.

"None. Just get out . . . Now!"

Eddie was moving towards the door, when Hilary said, "See you tomorrow, Eddie. And thanks for all your help."

Eddie looked from Hilary to Mr Wensleydale. It was always interesting when adults were about to do battle. These were like two stags squaring up to each other. Although it was his fate at the hospital that was teetering in the balance, he felt quite interested in what promised to be a rattling good argument.

"Tomorrow?!" blustered Mr Wensleydale.

"I asked Eddie to help with a baby rabbit that was left here this morning," said Hilary, calmly putting Miguel back in the aquarium.

"And why, may I ask, did you do

that?" asked Mr Wensleydale, with a little sneer on his face.

"Because he has been an enormous help to the nursing staff. Because he is intensely interested in the care and welfare of animals. And because I think this is precisely the sort of interest we should be encouraging," said Hilary.

"May I remind you that I have been working at this practice for considerably longer than you, Ms David," said Mr Wensleydale.

"Then you will fully appreciate all I've just said," Hilary pointed out.

"Will I indeed? Perhaps you should give up veterinary work and become a social worker, Ms David. I'll speak to you tomorrow morning when you've had time to reflect upon what you have done. And you . . . " He turned to Eddie, "One wrong move and you're out!"

With that, Mr Wensleydale stormed out, the little pink spots under his eyes having ballooned into great red blooms.

Eddie was gobsmacked, but he couldn't help clenching his fist and muttering, "Yes!"

Hilary David exhaled deeply.

"Good night, Eddie. And don't gloat. It was only a battle we won here. Not the war."

Maybe so, but it was a pretty dramatic battle. Even Eddie had never seen Mr Wensleydale so puffed up and angry. He wished he could have a photograph of his face. The important thing, however, was that he was allowed to come to the hospital. And he had Thumper. His Thumper.

Chapter Seven

A Big Loss and a Big Idea

In fact, Eddie was so excited about Thumper that he rushed round to see his best mate from school, Imran, to tell him about having his own rabbit.

"He's highly intelligent, probably one of the most intelligent rabbits around," said Eddie modestly.

"Oh, yeah, right," said Imran, who was inclined to be a bit cynical. "I suppose you sat him down at a computer and gave him an intelligence test. I suppose he can speak three languages and knows his twenty-six times table."

"Four, actually," said Eddie.

"What?" asked Imran.

"Thumper knows four languages. "Rabbit, English, and two others."

"What two others?"

"How should I know when I can't speak them myself, drongo?" said Eddie, pulling a face at Imran.

"Well, if you can't speak them, how do you know it's two? Maybe it's five, or seven."

This sort of conversation could go on for hours. It did.

The next day Eddie was at the hospital

before school, at lunchtime, and again after school. He fed Thumper and then went with Hannibal to see Bartholomew. The cage door was open. Squatting beside him and patting his head was a man Eddie hadn't seen before. Bartholomew looked awful. His nose was dry and, although he had eaten a little, his bowl was still two thirds full of food.

Eddie sat down next to the man.

"You his owner?" he asked.

"Yes. Tom Grayson."

"I'm Eddie. I come and see Bartholomew every time I'm here. His leg is getting better but he isn't. I wish he'd start to look livelier. Everyone's very puzzled about him."

"Yes. Poor old chap. Look at him. Breaks my heart it does."

"I used to see him on match days," said

Eddie. "Strutting around like one of those showground horses. Like he was proud of himself."

Tom laughed.

"That's right. Pleased as a parrot in a peanut factory. They'll miss him at the Cup Tie tomorrow. Very popular he is – with the team and the supporters."

"I bet he'll miss them too," said Eddie.

Eddie couldn't exactly be sure, but he thought he heard Bartholomew give a little groan.

"Do you think he knows about the Cup tie?" asked Eddie.

Tom looked at Bartholomew and rubbed his head. He was seriously considering the possibility.

"Shouldn't think so, but who knows what goes on inside his head? What I do know is that he's dropping a lot of weight. Can't understand it. Loved his grub. Specially on match days."

Tom gave Bartholomew a few more pats on the head and stood up to go.

"I'll be back tomorrow. After the match. Bye, old chap."

"I'll keep an eye on him for you," said Eddie.

The thought just would not go away: Bartholomew was miserable because he knew he was going to miss the match. Eddie couldn't explain how he knew, but he knew all right. He'd have a talk with Kate about it when he got home. He was just about to go when Greg called him into the side room. As he entered, Eddie knew Miguel was dead. He approached the aquarium and there was the body. It seemed much smaller, a husk. Eddie thought he'd feel sad. He usually did when animals died, and he'd learnt to respect the feeling; it was somehow necessary. But to his surprise, what he felt now was a powerful anger. He hadn't wanted to hold Miguel. In fact, he had found him a bit frightening, but he also knew that *he* would have found out how to look after him. Hilary David was right: some people liked the *idea* of having unusual pets, so they could swank around with them in front of their friends, but they couldn't be bothered to learn how to look after them properly. So they died. And here was Miguel – dead. And there was nothing anyone could do. Eddie found himself hoping that the owner, whoever he was, would know one day what it was like to be hungry and uncared for.

Eddie couldn't do anything to help Miguel, but he could to help someone else. He couldn't do it all by himself, so he'd have to use all his powers of persuasion. That night he told Kate his plan, and she smiled.

"Brilliant," she said. And that was all the encouragement he needed.

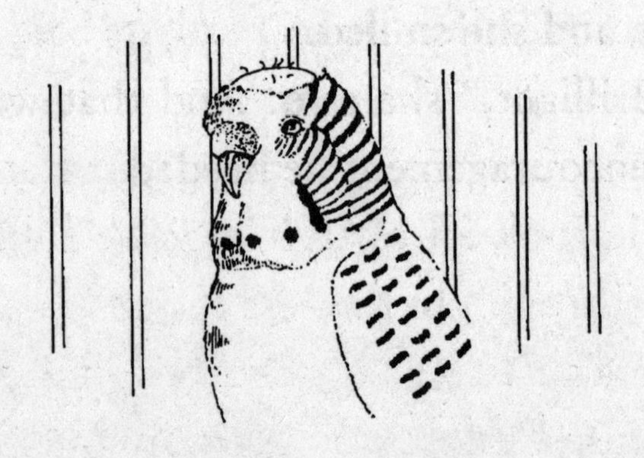

Chapter Eight

A Bit of Persuasion

"Absolutely not," said Ron the ambulance driver.

"But why not?" asked Eddie as they passed through Reception. A girl was holding a squirrel with a damaged leg. A woman was trying to get Chelsea to examine a puppy's ears. A man sat with two Welsh terriers, one on each knee. A man held a cage containing a budgerigar with no feathers on its head, its bald skull and pointed beak making it look like Eddie's Geography teacher, Mr Parkbin. Eddie took all of this in as he followed Ron through to the rest room.

"Because it's against hospital rules. Because I'd lose my job if anyone found out – which they would. Because it's a dopey idea in the first place. And because you're probably wrong. Need any more reasons?"

Ron leaned back and sipped his tea smugly. He'd won this argument. Or so he thought.

"If Bartholomew dies, it'll be all your fault," said Eddie with the most deadly serious expression he could muster on his face. He hated having to use blackmail like this, but desperate measures were called for. It was Saturday morning. There were only four hours to go. Ron looked at Eddie and frowned.

"He won't die. He's only got a broken leg – that won't kill him," he said.

"He's not eating much. His nose is all dry. He should be getting a bit of exercise by now otherwise his muscles will go all flabby. Hilary David said so. He's given up," Eddie said.

"You can't know that," said Ron.

"And you can't know he hasn't. At least we'd be doing something," said Eddie.

"Yes. Something that would lose me my job," said Ron and sniffed loudly to make the point even more clear.

"I suppose you're right," said Eddie. "It just seems such a shame, being so close . . ."

Ron eyed Eddie suspiciously.

"What are you on about now?" asked Ron.

"Oh. Nothing. Nothing at all to anyone who isn't a fan of Lymington United," said Eddie, knowing that whatever else Ron was, he was a big fan of Lymington United.

"If you're trying to say that we'll lose just because Bartholomew isn't there, you must think I'm off my chump," said Ron.

"Think about it," said Eddie. "First Cup Tie that Lymington has been in for years. They've played really well for the past two seasons. And when did they get Bartholomew as mascot?"

"Two seasons ago," Ron had to admit.

"I rest my case," said Eddie. "And when you're sobbing into your tea because they've lost, I'll try really hard not to say *I told you so*."

Ron's eyes flickered. He was hooked. For a moment, the glory of a Cup Tie win shone in his eyes.

"How would we get him out without being seen?" asked Ron – almost home and dry.

"I've worked it all out. We go through the back door and you bring the ambulance round. If we get caught I'll say it was all my idea and that I told you we had permission from the vets. I'll take the rap. Promise. What do you say?" asked Eddie, who already knew the answer. Whatever else was important in Ron's life, it would come second to football.

One hour later, Ron and Eddie crept into the ward to take poor Bartholomew to the football match. Anticipating Ron's eventual agreement, Eddie had already asked Kate and Imran to come along to help. It was now 1.30 p.m. and the three children were with Ron facing Bartholomew. Ron stood holding the trolley. Mr Wensleydale wasn't on duty until two, things were fairly quiet – it was now or never.

"That's one big poochie, Eds," said Imran, and he whistled through his teeth. "You said a dog, not a hairy bungalow. We'll need a crane to get him up on that trolley."

Eddie ignored Imran. He always exaggerated. Hannibal had come along to watch. Even Spock stopped grumbling to cast a beady eye down on the little group.

"Lose me job. Flippin' kids. What am I doing this for?" Ron was muttering as he knelt and held Bartholomew's mighty bottom.

Ron told them to roll Bartholomew

slightly to one side, so that he could slide the stretcher under him.

"For Bartholomew and for football," said Eddie.

"After three, and roll. One, two, three!" said Kate and they all tried to roll, taking particular care with Bartholomew's leg. Nothing. Bartholomew stayed exactly where he was. He hadn't moved even a centimetre. He still had his eyes closed as if he were completely indifferent to the whole affair. Almost as if it was happening to someone else.

"Told you," said Imran. "We need a crane. Never shift him – let alone lift him up onto the trolley."

"Why do boys always look on the worst side?" asked Kate. "You're a pacifist."

"Don't you mean pessimist?" asked Ron.

"She means pesky twit," said Eddie. "Now stop jabbering you lot, and start rolling. Come on. Try again."

Just to annoy everyone Imran started singing, "*Always look on the bright side of life*," as they tried to lift Bartholomew again. Useless. Worse than useless.

Eddie leaned down and lifted one of Bartholomew's giant ears.

"You're not being very helpful, Bartholomew," he whispered. "I'd really like it if you'd help. See, we're trying to get you to the Cup Tie. Your team needs you. A bit of effort on your part would be a help."

To everyone's amazement Bartholomew opened one eye and looked at Eddie. He seemed to be vaguely interested. Hardly a fireball of enthusiasm, but at least he was showing signs of life.

"Let me do it," said Ron, who, despite

his anxiety, had been enjoying watching the children fail to move Bartholomew. Now he could show young Eddie Wright how the professionals do it.

They stood back and with great expertise, Ron rolled Bartholomew slightly over and Imran and Eddie slid the stretcher under him. Ron gently pushed the dog the other way and with a mighty sigh and a grunt the large dog rolled over and onto the stretcher, where he lay on his back with his legs in the air, the broken one looking like a white flag of surrender. Imran started to giggle.

"Shut up!" hissed Eddie.

They all lifted the stretcher, which creaked and threatened to break, and just managed to get it onto the trolley. Ron sent Kate off ahead to act as lookout. The man and the two boys wheeled the trolley towards the back door.

Everything seemed to be going to plan. There was Kate with the door open, looking out. Then she ducked back inside just as they reached her.

"It's Mr Wensleydale! He's coming in the back," she whispered.

Chapter Nine

A Close Thing

Eddie looked at Ron.

"What are we going to do? If he sees me he'll go bananas," said Eddie.

Ron's gaunt face turned even more pale, his moustache drooping like a dying insect. He gulped, then strode out, just as Mr Wensleydale was reaching for the door. Ron quickly closed it behind him. The children backed the trolley down the corridor and into the store cupboard. Bartholomew lay on his back with his legs in the air, completely indifferent to the drama in which he was the central character.

Outside, Ron was struggling.

"Mr Wensleydale!"

"Hello, Ron."

"Glad I bumped into you," said Ron, smiling nervously.

"Why – what is it?" asked Mr Wensleydale.

"What's what?" asked Ron.

"I don't know. Did you want something? You said you were glad you bumped into me."

"Did I?" asked Ron. "Well, blow me down."

"I came in early because I've things to

do," said Mr Wensleydale, who was growing impatient. "What is it you want?"

"Ah," said Ron. "Ah, yes. It's . . . er . . . it's . . . the ambulance."

"What's wrong with it?" asked Mr Wensleydale.

"Oh. Nothing. Nothing at all. In fact. It's just been serviced and it's running very well. No problems there. I can quite safely say that the ambulance is running very nicely. And that's . . . that's what I wanted to tell you."

"You wanted to tell me that there's nothing to tell me about the ambulance?" snapped Mr Wensleydale.

"Yes," said Ron. "In fact, I could take you for a spin in it, so you can see for yourself."

"Ron. Do you ever have days when you think that everyone is mad except you?"

"Yes. Yes. I do," said Ron.

"Then you'll know exactly how I feel. Goodbye." And with that, Mr Wensleydale entered the back door of the hospital. Ron listened to the footsteps retreating inside, then leaned against the wall and breathed a sigh of relief.

A few minutes later the trolley was wheeled out.

"Almost cost me my job!" said Ron.

"No way," said Eddie. "You're too smart for that, Ron. Come on."

And what a strange sight it was. Bartholomew, legs in the air, being wheeled across to the ambulance. They lifted the stretcher from the trolley and into the back of the ambulance. Kate and Imran sat in the back with Bartholomew, and Eddie had the big treat of sitting up front with Ron.

FIRE EXIT
KEEP DOORS
CLEAR
IN CASE OF FIRE

"What's that button for?" he asked.

"Just leave it alone," said Ron, who was regretting ever getting involved in this.

"What does that switch do?" asked Eddie.

"Nothing."

"So it doesn't matter if I do this?" Eddie said as he pulled down the switch.

"Don't!" shouted Ron, but it was too late. The light on top of the ambulance started flashing and the siren wailed. Cars immediately started to pull over so that the ambulance could overtake them. Eddie was thrilled and in the back, Imran and Kate were cheering. Ron, who seemed to be sweating a great deal, leaned across and switched off the light and siren. He was starting to think that Mr Wensleydale was right – Eddie Wright was a bundle of trouble.

* * *

They got caught up in a traffic jam and no matter how much Eddie tried to persuade him, Ron refused to use the emergency light and siren. Eventually, they arrived at the football ground and drove right up to the main gate. The match had already started. Eddie jumped out and ran over to one of the security guards.

"Can you let us in, please?" asked Eddie.

"Tickets?" asked the man.

"We don't have any."

"Then you don't come in, do you?" said the man.

Eddie could hear the crowd roaring.

"What's the score?" asked Eddie.

"Lymington are down two nil."

Eddie's heart sank. Two nil!

"You've got to let us in," said Eddie.

"No I haven't," said the man.

"But look – it's an emergency. That's why we're in an ambulance."

The man looked.

"That's an ambulance for animals. As far as I know there are no sick elephants inside. No monkeys fainted from over-excitement. No hamsters, the victims of cruel and unnecessary tackles from behind. No—"

"You know Bartholomew, the team mascot?" Eddie interrupted.

"Yes."

"He's in the ambulance. We have to get him in. The team needs him."

"Yes, and I'm Billy the Kid. Look, son. Just buzz off and wait until you can afford a ticket."

"It's true! Come and see for yourself," Eddie insisted.

"Oh yes, and while I'm looking in the

ambulance your mates try to sneak inside the ground. N-O spells, Get lost!"

"We'll bring him out to show you, then," implored Eddie.

"You could bring out the Queen Mother in a skin-diving suit and I wouldn't let you in, sonny."

It was useless. Then Eddie had an idea.

"Will you put out a message on the tannoy, then? For Tom Grayson, Bartholomew's owner. Say that Eddie Wright from the hospital is waiting outside and it's an emergency."

The man looked uncertain.

"Please!" said Eddie.

"All right, but if you're having me on there'll be big trouble."

The man disappeared through a door and a few minutes later an announcement was made: "Will Tom Grayson please go to the main gate to see Eddie Wright from the Animal Hospital. It's an emergency."

And Eddie waited.

Chapter Ten

The Hero returns

Eddie listened to the crowd. Every time there was a roar he imagined that the opposition team, Hedley Rovers, had scored, and every time there was an "OOH!" or an "AH!" he thought that Lymington had almost scored. The minutes ticked by. Then Tom arrived, breathless. He looked very pale.

"Where is he? What's wrong with Bartholomew?" He asked, panting heavily, and looking at the ambulance.

"He's all right. Sorry, but I had to say it was an emergency to get you out here," said Eddie.

It was half-time and a moment arrived that has now entered footballing history. Lymington were two down. Supporters were eating hot dogs, drinking tea and cokes, moaning about the match if they supported Lymington, and saying what a great game it was if they were Rovers supporters. Nothing unusual in that. But what happened next was.

From the tunnel an ambulance drove slowly onto the pitch and into the centre of the field. The back doors were opened and three children, two boys and a little girl, and two men, one in a uniform, lifted a stretcher out onto a hospital trolley. On the stretcher was a large dog on its back with its legs in the air. A few people in the crowd recognised him. Whispers started. "It's Bartholomew." . . . "Hey! It's our mascot." . . . "It's Big Belly Bart!" . . . "Bart's back!"

Slowly, the whispers and shouts reached through the wall of Bartholomew's misery and slowly, very slowly, his ears twitched and pricked. An eye opened, then the other, and Bartholomew took in his surroundings. He couldn't believe it. He blinked. Eddie imagined that Bartholomew was thinking that he'd died and woken up in heaven: his beloved football ground. Now, more members of the crowd were cheering and a chant started, fairly quiet at first, then building to a crescendo:

BAR-THO-LO-MEW! BAR-THO-LO-MEW!

Bartholomew's tail twitched . . . then wagged a little . . . then wagged a lot, whacking Kate accidentally in the face and almost knocking her over, but, being the sort of girl she was, she thought this was hilarious and started laughing and dancing around, chanting: "Bar-tho-lo-mew! Bar-tho-lo-mew!"

Bartholomew rolled over and looked around.

"He wants to get down," said Eddie.

"But he can't!" said Ron.

"Who's going to stop him?" asked Imran.

Clearly no one was.

They all helped Bartholomew to get off the trolley, taking great care with his leg. Eventually he was standing all by himself, the cast on his broken leg taking

much of his weight. A breeze ruffled his coat and he looked as if he was smiling, in the way dogs do. The crowd roared at this personal triumph.

"Hurrah! Hurrah for Bart!"

As the players came back on the pitch Bartholomew managed to walk, quite slowly, towards them. Tom beamed and Ron scratched his head. As for Eddie, he knew he'd done the right thing. It was funny how what appears to be the wrong thing to do often turns out to be right. Life was very funny and strange, he thought, especially with animals. People were unpredictable, but animals were magic.

Chapter Eleven

DECEIVING CHEESY

Back at the hospital, Chelsea wasn't quite as elated as Eddie. In fact, she'd just had the shock of her life. She'd gone into the rest room for her tea break and switched on the television. There on the screen were her brother and sister in the middle of Lymington United football pitch, with

Imran, Ron and another man, the hospital ambulance, *and* Bartholomew, who should have been in the ward convalescing! She put down her tea before she dropped it and leapt from her chair as Mr Wensleydale entered. Chelsea just managed to stand in front of the screen before he saw the picture.

"Chelsea, do you usually watch television with your back to it?" asked Mr Wensleydale.

"No, no, of course not," she said. "It's just that it's not very interesting."

"Then switch it off," said Mr Wensleydale.

"Yes, I will," said Chelsea. "What a good idea. What a clever idea!"

"Yes, yes. What is the programme anyway?"

"It's . . . it's, er, a discussion programme about fashion. Very boring. Very dull.

You'd hate it."

"Then why are people shouting and cheering as if they're at a football match?"

"Are they?" asked Chelsea. "It's probably because the programme's almost finished. Everyone's glad it's over."

Mr Wensleydale looked troubled.

"They must be putting something in the water. Everybody here is going round the bend. Ron's brain clearly fell out without anyone noticing, and now you. What is wrong with everyone?"

Behind Chelsea, on the screen, nothing at all seemed to be wrong with Bartholomew. Even his leg was starting to feel better. He was slowly walking off the pitch, accompanied by his friends, and to the mighty roar of the crowd. Even with his leg in plaster, he looked like a champion. He certainly felt like one. The members of Lymington United football team looked at each other and, for the first time that afternoon, they started to believe they too might be champions.

Mr Wensleydale made himself a cup of tea, took a last look at Chelsea, and left to see what could be done about a Labrador with earache. You know where you are with animals, he thought. People are so unpredictable – which is precisely what Eddie thought, although it would have come as a shock to Mr Wensleydale to realise that he and Eddie had anything in common.

Chapter Twelve

A Glorious Victory

Eddie couldn't believe it. The change in Bartholomew was nothing short of a miracle. There they were, sitting in the Directors' Box, drinking coke and eating crisps, watching the match, with Bartholomew behaving like a king. People approached occasionally and gave him titbits and children came to sign his plaster cast. Bartholomew accepted all these favours with a regal grace. Occasionally he turned and gave Eddie, or Tom, or one of the others, a huge lick. It was all very wonderful. Only Ron looked uneasy.

On the pitch things were also starting to go very well indeed. Lymington had asserted themselves and scored one goal. Then another. And finally a third. The fans cheered. Eddie shouted his delight. Bartholomew barked and barked. Everyone was happy. Even Ron managed a smile. But now the match was over, there was a new problem. They had managed to get Bartholomew out of the hospital and to the match, but now they had to smuggle him back in without being seen.

* * *

At the hospital, Greg had discovered Bartholomew was missing and was about to report it to Mr Wensleydale when Chelsea told him what she guessed had happened.

"Your little brother certainly makes things happen, doesn't he? Right. We have to make sure Mr Wensleydale doesn't come into the ward until after they get back. If he looks as if he's heading this way, stop him."

"How?" asked Chelsea.

"Anything. Invent an emergency. Faint. Tell him a joke. Just stop him."

Ten minutes later, Mr Wensleydale was just about to check on the patients in the ward when Chelsea appeared.

"Mr Wensleydale, can I see you for a moment?" she asked.

"What is it?" he asked.

"It's . . . er . . . it's Hannibal. He's in Reception."

"So? He's often in Reception. What's wrong with him?"

"Best to see for yourself," she said.

Hannibal was fast asleep under Chelsea's desk, dreaming and snoring and snuffling when Chelsea and Mr Wensleydale approached and bent down.

"There," said Chelsea.

"He's asleep," said Mr Wensleydale.

"Yes. Exactly!" said Chelsea, as if this proved her point, whatever the point was.

"So he's asleep," said Mr Wensleydale, irritably. "Hannibal spends half his life asleep. It's a hobby with him."

"Ah," said Chelsea, "but not at this time of day. It's very unusual for him to be asleep at this time. So I thought there might be something wrong. I mean, perhaps he's running a temperature. Look at all that wetness around his chops."

"He's a bulldog!" said Mr Wensleydale, whose voice was getting louder. "Bulldogs are always slobbering. For goodness sake, they're like little slobber machines. It's how they're built! So what's the problem? And, what is going on here?"

Then he stopped. Everyone waiting in Reception was staring at him. Luckily, Kalim came hurrying in and asked Mr Wensleydale to come and examine a parrot with a sore throat. Chelsea breathed a sigh of relief.

Back at the football ground the victorious Lymington team members all helped to load Bartholomew back into the ambulance and waved goodbye as Ron put it into gear, and worried. What if Bartholomew's absence had been reported to the police? What if Mr Wensleydale discovered that he, Ron, had been directly involved? Never, never again, would he get caught up in one of Eddie Wright's wild schemes.

"Don't worry," said Eddie, beaming at Ron from the passenger seat. "Stay cool."

"I am," lied Ron. "Cool as a cucumber, me."

Chapter Thirteen

THE HEROES RETURN

Ron parked the ambulance at the back of the hospital. Kate and Imran went to make sure the coast was clear while Eddie and Ron helped Bartholomew down. Tom had stayed at the ground.

Unlike the uncooperative and miserable dog that had left the hospital,

Bartholomew was now feeling quite perky. He gave Eddie some enormous licks that almost took off his face, and when Ron was bending down to adjust the trolley, Bartholomew gave him a playful shove with his nose and sent him sprawling on the pavement. Eddie laughed and Ron scowled.

After his refreshing sleep, Hannibal was there at the back door to meet Eddie and offer a few encouraging licks. They got Bartholomew back to the ward without any trouble and Ron went off for a cup of tea.

"I bet that was your idea, Eddie," said Greg, as he got food and water for Bartholomew. "In future, tell someone what you're doing. If Chelsea hadn't seen the match on television we wouldn't have had a clue. I'm just thankful that Bartholomew didn't damage the leg."

"He's miles better!" said Eddie. "Just look at him."

Greg had to admit that this was a transformed dog as they watched Bartholomew wolf down his food and slurp a full bowl of water. His eyes had a sparkle in them and his coat had a sheen – all signs that this was a champion of a dog about to make a full recovery.

An hour later, Mr Wensleydale was convinced that everyone really had gone mad when he came into the ward and examined Bartholomew.

"He's making an excellent recovery," he said to Greg. "Obviously, all he needed was quiet and rest, no excitement. Why is he wearing a football scarf?"

"No idea," said Greg.

When Mr Wensleydale looked around, Greg was smiling to himself.

"What's so funny?" asked Mr Wensleydale.

"Funny? Nothing. Absolutely nothing," said Greg, smiling even more broadly. "As you say, Mr Wensleydale, no excitement."

Chapter Fourteen

A Special Honour

That evening there was a special event at the hospital. Hilary David had called all the staff and Eddie into the rest room. No one knew why exactly. Only Mr Wensleydale wasn't invited, not because Hilary didn't want him to be there, but because she could see no point in annoying him any further. He didn't want Eddie at the hospital and that was that. Everyone else did want him there. Certainly the animals did. Kalim, Greg, Ron, Chelsea and Eddie stood facing Hilary David as she began to speak.

"I want to say a few words to thank Eddie for the time he gives up to help us here at the hospital. We all know how we need more money, more staff, more of everything to keep things running as we would like, but what we mostly need is the sort of concern and care that Eddie shows when he's here. And he always manages to have a smile on his face, which is more than I can say for some. Eddie has also very kindly agreed to take particular care of the baby rabbit that was left at the hospital. Which is why I'd like him to accept this."

Hilary took a certificate from her

pocket and gave it to Eddie. He blushed as he read it.

This is to certify that

Eddie Wright

has been made a special friend of

Rainbow
ANIMAL HOSPITAL

Eddie beamed as everyone, even Ron, applauded.

Ten minutes later Eddie was holding Thumper and telling him about the football match and his certificate. The little rabbit twitched his whiskers and listened intently. Eddie knew that this was the beginning of a very special friendship.

Enjoy more great stories from

Trash Cat's Secret

"I thought tortoises were meant to be dead slow," said Eddie. "This one's more like Linford Christie."

Hilary David laughed at the female tortoise called Charlie, who was about the size of a saucer, lumbering for all she was worth across the X-ray plate. It surprised Eddie how quick and nimble a tortoise could be. Eddie caught her deftly in both hands and returned her to the centre of the plate. The owner of the tortoise had brought her into the hospital that morning because she had a lump on her neck and for the past ten minutes Hilary had been trying, unsuccessfully, to take an X-ray. Charlie refused to keep still. In fact, she was extremely angry, spitting and straining and hissing every time she was picked up and returned to the centre of the plate. The X-ray machine was the size of a large overhead projector, and kept in the prep room where animals were usually prepared for operations that would be done in the theatre next to it. Eddie sometimes watched different animals having parts of their bodies shaved in readiness, and saw the autoclave, a large oven-like machine in the corner, being loaded with instruments and bowls to be sterilised. He had not yet been allowed to watch an actual operation. But this tortoise who wouldn't keep still was another first.

"I could hold her," said Eddie.

"Then we might end up with an X-ray of your hand," said Hilary.

It was a problem. How could they keep Charlie still for a moment?

Eddie thought hard. Sometimes, if he had a real problem, he would say what it was to himself, not aloud but silently, then count to ten. If he was lucky, the solution appeared to plop into his brain like magic. He had picked up this trick from his little sister Kate, who, despite being only seven, seemed to have a vast knowledge of how the human brain worked. She was also a good fighter and a good laugh. The counting to ten didn't always work, but it was certainly worth a try. He tried it now. He said what the problem was, then counted, one, two, three, four, five, six, seven, eight, nine, ten.

"Sellotape!" he said.

"Excellent idea," said Hilary. Eddie held Charlie, while Hilary got some sticky tape from her office. She cut two long strips and crisscrossed them over Charlie's shell and onto the X-ray plate.

Charlie was furious. She spat and hissed and tried to use her powerful legs to free herself, but it was no use. Like it or not, there she was, stuck fast. Eddie moved behind the protective wall as Hilary lowered the hood of the X-ray machine. She stepped back to join Eddie, her thumb ready to press the switch at the end of the extension lead she was holding. The X-ray flashed on Charlie for a moment.

"There, you can put her in the ward now, Eddie, and when I develop the negative we'll see how big this lump is."

Eddie took Charlie back to the ward and put her in one of the cages fixed to the wall. In the cage below was a beautiful terrier dog, a golden colour with a thick fringe almost covering his eyes. It was his eyes that were the problem. Greg, the nursing assistant, was bathing them three or four times a day until surgery was performed. The dog, called Frisk, had a rare problem; his eyelashes curled over and grew into his eyes. If untreated, the dog could go blind, slowly and painfully.

Eddie tickled his nose through the wire of the cage, then went off to the smaller ward to see his rabbit, Thumper, for whom he had been given special responsibility until the rabbit was strong enough and an owner could be found for it. Of course, Eddie very much hoped that no owner would be found – ever. Although he didn't know it, all the staff at Rainbow Animal Hospital, except Mr Wensleydale, had agreed to keep Thumper as a permanent resident because Eddie had grown so attached to him. He was now several months old and, apart from being a little on the small side, seemed perfectly healthy. Eddie took him out of his hutch and gave him a kiss on the nose. Thumper licked Eddie's face enthusiastically. Eddie put him down and laughed as the rabbit lolloped round and round his feet.

Order Form

To order books direct from the publishers, just make a list of the titles you want and send it with your name and address to:

Dept 6,
HarperCollins Publishers Ltd,
Westerhill Road,
Bishopbriggs,
Glasgow G64 2QT

Please enclose a cheque or postal order to the value of the cover price, plus:

UK and BFPO: Add £1 for the first book, and 25p per copy for each additional book ordered.

Overseas and Eire: Add £2.95 service charge. Books will be sent by surface mail, but quotes for airmail despatch will be given on request.

A 24-hour telephone ordering service is available to Visa and Access card holders on 0141-772 2281.